The
of Twelve
Chimes before
CHRISTMAS

The Twelve Chimes before CHRISTMAS

ORION BLIGHTMAN

PARTRIDGE

To order additional copies of this book, contact
Toll Free 800 101 2657 (Singapore)
Toll Free 1 800 81 7340 (Malaysia)
orders.singapore@partridgepublishing.com

www.partridgepublishing.com/singapore

Contents

Let every breath be your last.
Let nothing ever come to pass.
Time ticks on, bits and pieces.
Moving on, but looking back
At memories, as they ride us home.

—*Orion Blightman*

Preface

Christmas is a time when everyone comes together to celebrate this joyous day. But as we immerse ourselves in carols and songs, what are the things we tend to forget in our lives? Alas, how could we remember something that we have already forgotten …

We move too fast in life and often do we forget the things that hold dear to us. But the snow remembers and the faraway town echoes in the distant snow, away from the world, waiting for the twelve chimes to ring across the town upon this cold Christmas Eve. Each chime holds a memory and a story to tell, written in poetry, a remnant of childhood and all that was good. However, none of these stories should you expect to be merry or fanciful.

So prepare yourselves as I bring you to the town that was once lost and forgotten, and the stories that I'm about to tell you may present to be sad and melancholy, but at the same time, they do retain heartfelt and warming moments that show us the meaning of Christmas. And perhaps, could we retrieve something meaningful as we move on in these sombre tales.

Now, be awaken from the sleep that is long overdue and remember the twelve chimes before Christmas.

The Twelve Chimes Before Christmas...

So this is where it all began
from a place where memories are long lost and forgotten.
A small town awakes upon this Christmas Eve
to sing the twelve chimes before Christmas.

For each new chime lies a chapter to behold
a story that we grew to live and forget.
In verse and rhyme these tales are told
to sing the twelve chimes before Christmas.

The soldier boy who kept his silence
to a father who carried his will.
The little match girl who kept her light; all
to sing the twelve chimes before Christmas.

But these tales you hear are not for the blessed,
nor in dreams shall you find solace and peace.
So brave yourselves in these sombre tales
and sing the twelve chimes before Christmas.

Chapter 1

The Soldier Boy

Upon this snowy winter's night,
the storm raged on, so ashen and cold.
The wind blew stronger, and every second it grew
until nothing could be seen but a shade of fearsome hue.
Yet there it was,
among black trees and shadows.
A silhouette of a boy came walking through the deep, deep snow.

He was a weak little boy in fours and twos,
barely managed with his ragged clothes on.
His chest was pale and left uncovered
as his breath was brief in the frostbitten air.
Half-a-door's height, he moved through the snow,
but the snow that grew reached up to his waist,
forcing him to turn from this treacherous place.
But he knew where he was going.
He knew when to stop.
"Almost there," he said to himself
as he marched on quietly
past the old bench
and the little girl in red.

It was not long until he reached the town.
He could feel the cold stones under his feet.
A vast course of snow led on far in the distance,
with glowing streetlights guiding the way.
Houses built on two sides of the road
were carved with numbers on red bricks and gold.
The lights were bright, and soft carols
came pouring through bedroom windows.
But the little boy marched on, steadfast and true.
"Almost there," he said to himself
as he stumbled along the familiar road
of tiny footsteps
on the cold and painted snow.

The little boy came to an end of the path
and stopped at a house of red, white, and green.
A Christmas wreath was hanging on the alder wood door;
a candle in the center stayed unlit.
But it smiled, so gently, at the weary little child
as the boy walked up the doorsteps
and knocked three times
on the old alder wood door.

Who could it be?
But there was no reply.
The lady in the simple dress hurried to the door
to find a skinny little boy
kneeling at her doorstep, freezing and half-alive.

She quickly brought him in
with clean clothes and heat,
and a fireplace to keep the young boy warm to his feet.
She was a kind, loving lady and a mother of three,
working day and night, from one house to another,
never complaining nor thinking that
one day she could leave it all behind
for she has three spirited girls to come home to.
And on this day of Christmas Eve,
a fine feast of turkey and bread was to be prepared
for her three lovely daughters:
Liz, Tess, and June.
But she pitied the small boy
with his bony fingers and faded cheeks,
so she offered him a slice of that rich Christmas meat.

The room was smaller than what it might seem
but brighter and warmer than any house could give.
The windows were crested with holly and mistletoe,
with the occasional complements of white frosted snow.
And a lovely pine tree that sat next to the fireplace
was decorated with pretty ornaments
of hearts red and blue.
"What is your name?" asked the kind mother.
But the little boy sat there
and kept his words.
Crossing his hands against his will,
He looked in to the flames

that danced his memories far, far away.

The room was louder when the three girls woke.
First came the youngest, the three-year-old, who
came running across the room to find her dear mommy.
Then the second one rushed in
to see whether Santa came earlier this special year.
Liz, however, was tired and sleepy;
yet she still came, like an elder sister would.
But the three girls were shocked
by the pale little boy who sat
near the fireplace, so ragged and grey.
And so the mother led off a cheerful smile
as she set the table with forks and knives,
"We'll have an early Christmas this year,
so let us feast tonight!"

The house was filled with laughter and joy,
especially with the company of the skinny little boy.
And oh how the family feasted!
Although there was not much—
a drumstick of a turkey and a fresh loaf of bread—
but enough for the girls and their mother in plain dress.
The big sisters helped each other with their humble plates
and carried the Lord's Prayer with thankfulness and grace,
while the little one,
already started munching on happily
with her slice of juicy roast,

stuck her fingers inside her mouth
and licked them one by one for a final taste.
And, of course, the little boy joined the table,
nibbling on the piece of golden bread so generously given
as he listened to the three girls
sing for the storm to pass away.

The storm subsided, and the meal was long done.
The girls were asleep, and the house was quiet.
It was time for the little boy to leave.
As he stood up and walked towards the door,
the kind mother gave him an old leather jacket
and spoke to the little boy in a gentle voice,
"It belonged to my husband, who was lost in war.
It stayed by him for many years,
guiding him back to our lovely home.
But now it needs an owner,
and one you should take
as a parting gift to guide you back
to where you belong and your rightful place."
The little boy accepted the mother's gift.
He turned and smiled for the very first time
at the woman who bade him goodbye,
now younger and lovelier than before.
And went off into the cold and lonely night.

It was not long until he left the small town, retracing
his faltering steps back to the beginning,

where the snow was deeper
and harder to advance.
He arrived at the bench that he
once passed and the girl in red, who was
now nowhere to be seen.
He lay on the bench with his leather jacket on,
and he faced towards the town for the very last time,
a lonely speck in the deep, deep snow.

The air was thinner and colder now.
The first bell chimed at the heart of town,
and the radiance of the moon
blessed the town with a veil of phosphorescence and white.
The soldier boy called upon the beauty of the night
as he returned, once again, to this homely place
of black trees and shadows
and never-ending sleep.

Chapter 2

A Father's Will

The world was estranged at least
for a moment when he was asleep.
Or was he?
The weary man slept with his work boots on.
And a bottle, half-empty,
sat by the dim bedroom windows,
looking out on the empty streets of the city
once lost and forgotten.

Just another day, only
it's Christmas Eve.
The man struggled his way up
and kept his gnarly hands to his face.
Wrinkled as they were old,
those hands never belonged to a man at his forties.
A pair of woodcarver's hands,
but a mere amateur; a skill
that he determined to learn
a couple of years back on this very day.
The man never thought he could stay for this long.
Perhaps away from this old town
to a faraway city he so dreamed of when he
was young.

But he never left.
For he met the girl he always loved
and a son
to come home to
and adore.

Life, however, was not as hopeful
or merciful when the mother was too young to be taken
from childbirth, and the father who watched
as his loving wife slowly slipped away by his side.
For many days and nights, the father cried,
but never was he given solace and peace.
Only their child gave him comfort
with his yearnings of sweet milk and soft, tender sleep.
Then, on a Christmas Eve as cold as this,
the boy got ill at the age of five.
A terrible cold that grew to his lungs
tormented the poor boy with a burning fever
and was never woken since.
But the father kept to his word
and stayed by his beloved boy.
And this night, as any night before,
he took his only coat
and went out into the bitterly cold snow.

The streets were empty on this stormy night
but considerably warming
With candlelights glowing from their little red houses.

And for a moment,
he thought he was asleep.
Whispers hushed ever so faintly
But audible to the man beyond the dust and snow.
Or was he hearing soft carols floating
in the distant wind?
The freezing air dulled his senses.
The storm grew behind him,
covering his footsteps like
a shadow in the mist.
But soon he arrived at the crossroad
and the little tavern sheltered between
Jill's restaurant and the old barbershop.

"The usual?" the woman behind the table asked
as she offered him a light green bottle
with a small glass cup waiting to be filled.
Yet the lonely man just sat there, legs crossed,
on the uneasy stool,
waiting.
As he looked at the empty glass before him,
A temptation came over him, enough to free him from his
pains.
It could be done in a simple movement.
Only temporary,
but enough for the lonely man.
He missed his memories, and this place reminded him
of that same feeling which was once lost and forgotten …

Home.

The only thing that meant right in his life

as a father.

Yet he never poured a single drop,

and the cup was never filled

for the lonely father had to move on.

He stepped back again into the howling night and

left the world of spirits and warm, fading lights.

He bargained his coat at the barbershop next door

for a pair of silver blades and a penny or two.

Then he rushed off to Jill's for a piece of mincemeat pie

and a simple match

from the little girl in red.

But the song of grace echoed in the distance

as the writhing storm had now taken its place and grew

fiercer than ever.

Voices emerged like scattered shadows from cracks

of broken alleys

and gushing waters.

Begone!

A silent grave awaits for the unsound mind.

The brave father held onto his chest

as the angel led the way in the deep, deep snow.

The loving father returned to his empty house

and approached the wooden bed

where his little boy slept.

He lit the candle beside him with the only match.
The boy showed no color but peaceful in his sleep
like a mirror of water reflecting no stars.
But a light filtered through the boy's pale skin,
cold yet so alive in his father's eyes.
Or was it just the candle and its enkindled light?
The father brushed against his forehead, just to
see him clearly underneath the frozen cast;
His son remained unmistakenly his son.

There was never a moment in life did the father
feel at peace. And time was, as if,
slower and much more of a memory
in the making, but nonetheless,
trickling away ever so slightly. The father
carefully trimmed the boy's curled hair
with the new scissors he got. Then he took out a paintbrush
and some old paint from his broken drawer.
He painted the boy's lips with a light currant pink
and his eyebrows with a tint of amberwood brown.
Then on both cheeks, a dash of red and tender peach
to give them life, and that one little thing they called Love;
the father gave them color.
And for a moment;
his son was lively and whole again.
With the flame still enkindled
and the night was still young,

he watched over the little boy
on the precipice of longing and wild haunted dreams.

The candle fell to its last moments
as the second chime rang at the center of town.
The last flame slowly faded into the night,
leaving behind a trail that follows
and the father's last breath beside the silent tomb.
It was then, for a moment;
he saw his little boy smiled at him for the very first time:
ever so slightly …
ever so gently …
But it was all enough for the loving father
to see the world for one last time
and the town once lost and forgotten …
The world was estranged
as did the first snow fall on the day of Christmas.

Chapter 3

The Waiting (Part 1)

Upon the depths of fretful snow,
the green buds settled amongst the cold
and sleep, waiting for that
one moment to be woken up by those powdered
memories of longing and love.
Snowdrops bowed like silent prayers
where time and time again,
do these destined lovers cross paths
upon the vile intersections of life
and shared little attention to what their lives could lead them;
away from their town
and each other of whom they love.

Twenty years in the city could change a man,
and indeed, do these times
keep him very much in a world of endless repetitions
and empty emotions; a prisoner
of one's fate and fatherly expectations.
Who could have thought life was given with such painful
rhetorics?
Alas, of one that's beyond our reach, who is to say?
But to write on credits and debits …
(as if these graphs and numbers mean anything useful.)

What is more a dream than one that's forgotten
when you open your eyes? For it was
in the first few seconds
did the man find himself in mournful tears, trying to find
that loss of nothingness to fill his empty heart.
But the longer he stayed awake,
the further he felt the currents were no longer real ...
The cold in the floors grew tangible to his feet,
as he, himself was awake and clear
to move himself for another day.
And today was the day that he could never forget,
for Christmas Eve
is the day to love ... and to remember.

The city was never livelier tonight
with soft patches of snow and fancy neon lights.
Looking at the buildings that spiraled into the skies,
it could make one gaze in awe of the many possibilities
that these bright monuments would give us homage to the
riches and kings.
Alas, that is what we live for, is it not?
Yet do these crowded streets and noble white collars
present themselves nothing more
than just fleshy decors ...
The snow fell gently in the lonely night
as the green bulbs bloomed in the near distance:
The balcony of the young man's flat.

Snowdrops—
drooped like bell-shaped petals,
painted in the crescent and powder snow.
A white so humbled within a mirror of three
and six smaller petals to cover all facets of the heart.
Its scent carries a green taste by the palate,
a mild sweetness flew through the air
as the winter winds caressed the white drooping bells
that sang lost whispers of story and song.
But it meant something more to the young man
for that light perfume did give him peace.
Was it a dream that he forgets where he belonged?
The man could vaguely remember.
But perhaps the snowdrops did remind him of a lullaby
from that distant old town he left so long ago
and a promise that kept him waiting in the deep, deep snow.

So the man left in his heavy coat
as he followed the snowdrops into the wild withering snow.
He knew not what he was doing, but
his heart grew more certain for every step he took
was like a thread following its own embroidery
and the calling of a chariot
to bring him home
through haunted woods and dark twisted roads.

It was not long until he reached an opening,
and there, stood before him

the remains of an old town that still kept its solitude
amongst the cold and snow.
There is a homely feeling to those little red houses
as he rode by, and the lights
that shone through those tinted windows
gave him more than just warmth but a humble courtesy
that he had always longed for, and more …
The snowdrops guided the way.
As the snow grew fervor in the distant wind,
the little white buds did bloom to existence
in the little garden beside the old chapel and bells.

The man got off at the interaction across the road
and followed the grey path before him.
Lined on two sides of the path, the snowdrops
bowed to their mirrored opposites as if to give light
to those who passed them by.
The world was subdued in a single gasp
as the bed of white candle buds rose to the infinite,
breathing their first breath in the cold frosted snow.
It was then when the man found himself
standing amongst all faded memories
which he had come to forget and the sweetness in the air
that had once kindled his heart. Love was the dream
that's kept away from reality, but real enough
to be seen in the deep deep snow;
A wooden bench and the little footprints that led him here.

The winter was young in the first patch of snow
and without the slightest err to doubt
such simple love between a girl and boy. For their hearts
grew amongst those wishful snowdrops
as they met one snowy evening by the old wooden bench.
It only took a smile to be closer than friends
and every day in the garden where they
played and danced to fall in love.
He had always loved her smile
and how her eyes did reflect back to his …
How could he forget?

The man sat on the cold bench and watched
as the memories withered away in the dust and snow.
Twenty years in the city could change a man
and indeed, the boy was too early to be sent away
to distant lands and plucked from the very soil
which made him whole … his father made it certain.
It was all but a dream.
The snowdrops turned away in sullen tears
as the man left the wistful garden
and returned to the crossroad of red bricks and stone.

When the storm had passed, the world was frozen
in a moment of blissful tranquility
as the waiting came to a final stop.

"Hello, cold weather is it?"
    "Yes it is. Quite the storm."
"What brings you here?"
    "A dream of a silly man."
"Found what you're looking for?"
    "Yes. And I was … too early."

The young man and woman waited by the open road
as the third chime rang in the distant air,
echoing through the town like
an awakening from the fever dream
that kept them here
amongst the deep deep snow and
that one promise two kids made one snowy afternoon—
Now … but an epiphany of what it can be
and could only be:
a faded memory
at the brink
of fantasy and reality.

Chapter 4

The Waiting (Part 2)

Upon the depths of fretful snow,
the green buds settled amongst the cold
and sleep, waiting for that
one moment to be woken up by those powdered
memories of longing and love.
Snowdrops bowed like silent prayers
where time and time again,
do these destined lovers cross paths
upon the vile intersections of life
and shared little attention to what their lives could lead them;
away from their town
and each other of whom they love.

The faithful girl, who married at the age of 18
devoted her life to a complete stranger
but yet, it was done and
done without a chance to breathe
the sweet air and the snow that waltzed so freely in
the distant wind. Who is this man of silver rings?
She never knew even after all these years.
Marriage was a cruel thing to be surrounded by
gold and precious treasures
that meant nothing more to the poor girl but cold walls

that kept her here; a servant,
no more and no less.

What is more a dream than one that's forgotten
when you open your eyes? For it was
in the first few seconds,
did the girl find herself in mournful tears, trying to find
that loss of nothingness to fill her empty heart.
Many a night did the poor girl stay awake in her lonely bed …
Afterall, the man of silver rings
tends to sleep on his own. He never hurt her,
but he never loved her either. And for a girl
who was so young and lively, it was such a waste …
And this night of Christmas Eve, she woke again
in tears, cowering in her shadow. Why is she here?
There was no purpose and those rediculous chores
were but for mindless fools who believed in the making
of daily necessities that require supervision and duty;
all but man-made ideals that meant nothing
and changes through time.
Time was the only real thing that the girl believed in
which kept her moving
and waiting …
a silent promise.

Snowdrops – some say it could never be compared
to the passion of roses, nor the charm
of grand orchids. Humility was its own chastity

for the quiet snowdrops were the subtle beauty
that blooms in the night and forthcoming snow.
Withdrew in their shells, they waited patiently for that
one moment to be awake and notice
by those who had forgotten and lost in oblivious sleep.
The snowdrops guided the way
and its scent grew as far as it could reach,
riding on winter winds from the edge of the old town
to distant cities of land and sea; a unique fragrance
that taste of fresh pastures and a sweet that lingers
by the corner lip like a kiss
to remember and forget.

The girl remembered. She had always
remembered the snowdrops praying in the little garden
by the old chapel. In fact, she had always looked
forward to this day to be woken from
her long and miserable dream. This moment was real.
She was the girl who waited for twenty years
and every year in Christmas Eve, she would look
into the snow, the very snow where she met
the boy she loved. And his eyes would always
reflect back to hers … How could she forget?

A storm was coming, and the snow
grew thicker on the old window glass;
the only fragile thing that stood between cold worlds
and the fireplace. Yet what was the difference?

For her heart was cold and withering away
where the fire could not reach … the warmth
was on the other side in the cold and fretful snow,
buried deep within the white candle buds,
waiting to be lit. But perhaps it was just her
and that she was always too late as it was
in the first snow when she never said goodbye to the boy;
she was always too late and too scared … so she took
the latter, waiting for every Christmas Eve
and every Christmas Eve that is to come. But why would he
come?
He never did. And perhaps … He never will.
The wishful snowdrops quivered in the deep deep snow.

She loved the way how he looked at her:
The first glance was always the most precious
for his eyes would glow and that she would smile.
In fact, the promise was made not be spoken
but to be shown from a simple glance and
smile in return. It was by this silent promise
they knew they would see each other one day
even if they were apart. Love was the dream
that's kept away from reality, but real enough
to be seen in the snow beyond broken windows and curtains …
And upon the blessings of time, the snowdrops
bloomed all at once in the little white garden.

She left the house and arrived at the intersection,
just enough to see the white candle buds
in their iridescent glow as they danced in pairs
along the grey path. The blizzard raged
beyond the iron gates but the garden remained
undisturbed and ever so peaceful as if
time was still and kept in that very moment
in the frost and painted snowdrops.
The old bench sat in the center of the garden
but there was no one to be seen …
only two matches stayed unlit on the cold wooden stool
and the little girl in red faded in the distance.
Of course, why would he be here? The foolish girl
stood in the lonely garden as the gentle wind
brushed away those silent tears on this Christmas Eve
and the many Christmas Eves that were before.
The garden remained and the moment
stayed unchanged. She was always too late.
So the girl left the garden and the memories
that kept her waiting as she braved herself
in the cold and everlasting snow.

When the storm had passed, the world was frozen
in a moment of blissful tranquility
as the waiting came to a final stop.

"Hello, cold weather is it?"
     "Yes it is. Quite the storm."
"What brings you here?"
     "A dream of a foolish little girl."
"Found what you're looking for?"
          "Yes. And I was … too late."

The young man and woman waited by the open road
as the third chime rang in the distant air,
echoing through the town like
an awakening from the fever dream
that kept them here and could only be:
a faded memory at the brink
of fantasy and reality …
But when the fourth chime rang through
the garden of dreams, the man and woman
did turn to see: a final glance from the boy
who had gone so far away and the return of a smile
from the girl who waited and was always too late.

Chapter 5

Halfway

Halfway, was the wooden door
that stood between the fireplace and snow.
As we brave ourselves into the mist
and the unknown that awaits us on the other side,
we listen to the voices that whisper
in the deep deep snow … for halfway
was the point of unbecoming. The fear
to look back and down the road that forced us uncanny
do put us in a state of frenzy. Crude as it were,
the moment becomes unclear
as we live our lives as mist, but merely
not knowing the fact that we've never been born.
Worn and unclothed, the old man
sat by the doorstep and watched as the
first snow fell on the night of Christmas Eve.

Who am I amongst the town covered in snow?
For the man was just like any other,
only older and insignificant as the dust
among hundreds and thousands of crystallized silver
in the cold winter night. So was his purpose
of which he has none. That's what he was
tonight as the many nights before

and yet he sat there, unscathed and alone.
Oh how he cursed himself for being alive …
For it was 'till death do us part'
that became more than just a scythe to the heart.
He mourned for a holy matrimony that never lasted
and those haunting moments
in the bitter cold that kept him awake at night …

Then fell on his shoulder, a crow
griped its claws into the old man's skin.
Burnt marks grew in size and numbers
and deeper than the ones before. He had lost count.
Every day, he would carry wood
and deliver them to every red house in the town,
back and forth from his tiny store.
Hard work, but it was worth the pains
for he looked forward to the last stop: Home.
He would always be welcomed with a warm smile
to sit down and rest on his loyal chair.
He loved his wife. He loved the mild brew
that sat on the table beside;
The slight grittiness of the ceylon tea
and the rare sweetness at the end
by the white silver tips
that always let him sleep so peacefully at night.
But when he returned to the same doorstep alone,
he could only hide his eyes
from the rest of the world, squinting

those deep solemn pits in mournful tears …
as the snow casted its shade
along with these memories
that drifted so far away …

A storm was gathering in the restless snow
and it was within moments when the town
was covered in frost and dust.
There was a grave at the cemetery
on the far side of town where broken bones
clamored by the old cypress yew
like soft carols in the wind.
The roots ran deep beneath the ground
and the old man could feel it moving
ever so slightly as the wooden door
rustled in the cracks behind him …
The old man closed his eyes
as the sirens howled amist the snow,
retrieving what it seemed to be
the calling of a dying man …
for words were barely spoken in paper
and stone but only through windows
could you hear them whisper in the deep deep snow.

It was halfway at the eye of the storm
when she appeared in the depths of snow;
A little girl in red. She stopped when she saw him
and sat beside the lonely man. Who was she?

The little girl kept to herself as she
scurried away in the shadows
and the red hood that covered her face.
It only took a glimpse for the old man to see
beneath those gentle curls and realize how young
the girl was under her little red cloak.
Perhaps six or seven of age, but old enough
to know her way. Afterall,
she was just a painted shadow. Or why
would a little girl be wandering in this frightful snow?

It all came down to a single moment when
two unwonted souls collided upon broken worlds
whilst the stars above reflect those scattered underneath;
the little girl in red could only be
an imagination for the cold and unhinged mind.
She wasn't real … but it didn't matter—
for the old man welcomed the unexpected visitor.
The friendly strangers sat on the old staircase
as the snow rustled against the wind.
But the little girl didn't speak,
not even a word, and yet
she smiled at the old man as if
to comfort him for the many times that he hid
in those soulful eyes … and at last,
the old man was home
as the first tear fell upon his cheeks;
He cried for the moments of empty regret …

He cried for the kindness that kept him at work …
He cried for the love that never lasted, but knowing that
she will always be with him in his heart …

As the moment faded away, the town
returned once again to a world of chaos and cold. It was time.
The little girl in red gazed upon the snow
that led no paths and followed deeper into the storm
as paved for her; the storm guided the way.
And before she left, she gave the old man a match;
an ordinary match, but different
than the ones in her pocket. It was smaller
and bare without the bright red coating;
A burnt splinter that had served its purpose.
The charcoaled little thing looked at the old man
and bowed before him. He smiled.
A blue flame sparked in front of his eyes
as the little thing danced in his palm
Like music in water. And among the recurrence
that emerged and submerged
was a moment kept in another time … "You know,
She was always such a a good dancer."
The little girl stopped. It was then
when the old man heard
the gentlest voice and it gave him peace.
There were no words, only
three gentle knocks on the old wooden door.

When the storm has passed, the snow
settled upon the earth as it cascaded
from the mountains to the silent town below.
The sirens withdrew from its calling
while midnight chimes rang through the streets
like an old song. The headstones
were covered with a layer of snow
and the man on the doorstep
did close his eyes as the winter winds
blessed him with a soft faded kiss.
Halfway, the old man left the house
with the little match that did give him warmth
as the fifth chime rang on Christmas Eve.
The yew kept its words
and the old man drifted away
in the air of lost thoughts and dreams.

Chapter 6

The Blind, the Crooked, and the Halfman

The cold was merely a desolate place, where
One could remain undisturbed. And for one to long
for such a void seemed unnatural. It was
not the loneliness that killed a man,
but the prolonged bitterness that leads on forever
and the regret that was never to become
feasted upon the flesh of the misfortuned soul... and yet
were these discarded bodies and missing parts
still left with functional minds and
were consumed and twisted
upon the passing of time—
never to be seen as equals as those who lived
a simple and normal life;
for this is the malignity of deformed souls
at the altar of recrimination.
And in the little hut
where the monsters lie, the Blind,
the Crooked and the Halfman
drank to forget the night
that was stolen from them one Christmas Eve.

Of all the streets and houses that lived in the light,
one was stayed unlit and the other

was forgotten on the far side of town; for only
monsters lurk in the darkest of night …
"Monsters, they say! And monsters
we are! Look at you my blind old friend.
By god if I look any closer, I swear I could
see flies coming out from those pit-holes
of yours! And you, poking around with your broken stick,
if you could walk any slower, you'd
be first to freeze when you step out this door!
And then there's me, the devil's child, oh
Pray to your gods and curse me with words most foul
as if I give a damn to your precious scorns
or my worthless life to be called a mistake … I am."

The little man stumbled across the room
and back again, trying to steady his stubby feet.
The two older men watched as their
short friend surrendered to his ailing impulses.
But they didn't mind his painful words
or mad impulses because he was
always that way— every day
when a tear came falling from the corner of his eye
and he would cover it, why,
how could he show it? To be ashamed,
laughed at, hated upon …
He would never give them the satisfaction.

"My dear friend,
as much a deformity you agree you are,
it doesn't take away the gist
of your play. For you did choose
to play the long game as the three of us did.
And oh my small friend while as long
as you may live, my bones
would break like glass with a single fall.
And perhaps, it wouldn't matter at all.
For if my leg was made of snow and dust,
the other would be the wind
that's against the snow and the stick—
would be the space between that keeps them at bay."

The three-legged man took a sip from his cup
and moved himself from the bed to the table.
One could hear the clear knocks beneath the wood
and the unusual gallops that would keep them
entertained as he walked across the room.
"The Crooked", they called him; for a monster
deserves a better name and the man
was more than just a one-legged cripple but of one
hell-bent to see the satire in mind
and the mind was better crooked to see;
the feud of calm waters and the guile of broken things.

The storm made its way to the far side of town
and covered the little hut where the monsters

lie in darkness as the raging snow
devoured every last bit of light in the room.
Sometimes one could hear the monsters
breathing heavily against their chests and the sudden
hysteria they would let out from their lungs
as it surged thorugh the town in the wind and severed air.
The two monsters drank from their only cup
and continued insulting each other to their unholy putrescence;
A sick joke they played together but not at all serious.
For they knew it was not their fault
to be the lesser, only that life was much more
difficult and futile for them and the stares
didn't make it easier. "So to hell with them!
And damn to our lives and us,
monsterous beings!" "Hear hear!
My short repulsive friend. But what of you,
my quiet fool? you never spoke a word."

The creature sat in the corner.
It didn't move. It didn't speak.
It just nodded at the other two
and went back to its lonely space. For a monster,
he was the quietest of all. But when it comes
to being neglected and feared, his empty
eye sockets were enough to speak all tales of pain
and loneliness; he wasn't just blind,
his eyes were taken away. But it was not
the only thing that was stolen from him that night …

He brushed off the cobwebs and cleaned off
the dust on his arms and his face.
Then he sat up on his bed
and looked at his friends. But what he said next
held the monsters by their tongue:
"It's Christmas Eve, yes?"
"Yes, my blind friend. What about it?"
"Do you still remember your names?"

I haven't forgotten.
That was the answer they were expecting
themselves to reply, but they knew
their lives were never the same
and their names were indeed forgotten, casted away
in memories when they were still …
Human. They knew that they were different;
The Halfman who was born a dwarf
was abandoned by his parents and never had a choice.
The Crooked who lost his leg also lost
his only family and soon his mind.
At last, the Blind fool, whose eyes were taken
by a man, who also took his mother
and left him behind in a world that shared no light.
Then it was one Christmas Eve when these broken souls met
and pitied each other with their own damned fates.
For that was the night when these three vowed
to be monsters in hiding from the world and themselves …

Do you still remember your names?
The gentle snowdrops swayed in the distance
as the wind took those words away …

When the storm had passed through the empty town,
the streets returned to its former silence.
And outside the little hut where the monsters lie,
a light shone through the window: a candlelight.
It was at that very moment, the three monsters
saw each other's faces for the very first time
and the room was filled with empty tears.
John, Mark and Paul sat together at the table and talked
about the people that they were once before …
and they will remember
upon this night of Christmas Eve
and among all monsters that haunt in the night,
the sixth chime rang at the far side of town;
where three friends lived in a quiet little hut
and found themselves welcomed at a place called: Home.

Chapter 7

The Silver Cross

Beyond the bright walls of the forgotten town,
the shadows lurked amidst the cold and snow.
As the night grew darker, the nightmares came.
Don't fight; for it is easier to give in than to
listen to the silence that swirled through the air
like a deafening plague as it overcame our voices
and conscious minds ... the snow showed no mercy.
But there was one exception that ruled them all
that haunts at night and stalks in the day;
a remnant of the past that feeds upon regret
and one that sought forgiveness but the price
was too much to pay ... for time has no waiting.
Out in the storm of this Christmas Eve, the chapel
shone brighter than any house in town. And yet,
the ailing priest sat silently at the altar
as he drank the night away with his precious wine.

In what pleasure does a priest find in his wine?
Perhaps to seek enlightenment at the bottom
of an empty glass? Or was it just the flaw of human nature
to succumb to these unholy desires? No.
For there was nothing in the world could quench
the thirst of an alcoholic and even Bacchus's wine

could never fill a man's guilty heart. He had fulfilled his duties
in the candlelight service with prayers and songs
and now, as the wind raged beyond
these painted walls … he was just a man;
a lesser man among all faithful saints and the One above.
But on this night of Christmas Eve,
there was a visitor and he showed himself in
with a clever click: A thief.

As he creeped in the hallway and walked
towards the assembly of gold and silver,
he stopped when he saw the drunken priest
lying on the wooden steps in front of the altar.
The snowdrops whispered in the distance.
"Begone, young man! This is the house of the Lord
and 'tis unwise to steal. Heed my words
for the price is your soul. And if you do persist
in following this unwanted path,
it could only give you nothing but sin and misery.
So I pray you, awake from this foolish act
and live your life anew before it's too late."

"Ordained a priest yet none of which that follows.
Alas, rules were bounded like iron chains
and shan't be removed by some inscrutable excuse.
And yet you stand before his altar,
bathing in wine and the lies that you tell yourself
and others that listen to you.

You are as much as a liar, as I am as a thief."
The priest steadied his way up
and leaned on the long bench in front of him.
He could feel the pulse in his head
beating against his heart and he fell on his knees
with his back against the cross.
The thief stood tall by the podium as he watched
the drunken priest managed himself on the bench
and continued drinking away with the wine he had left …
The storm rattled against the doors
as the howling spirits roamed on the other side
in the vile depths of snow.

"Give me that." The thief snatched the wine holder
from the ailing man and took a large gulp
of the medicine. He sat next to the priest
and glanced at the gold and silverware on the altar;
The silver cross shone brightly in the candlelights.
The priest looked at the young man and noticed something
different to this common thief. He had no mask,
wearing only his pale face and the balaclava
of his identity that was kept secret. One thing he knew;
the man was not from around town, but one in search
for something in this cold and forgotten place.
The storm raged on in the bitter cold
as the two guilty men
stood in judgement before the holy cross.
Their shadows were deafened from their sight

and how they were too afraid
to look back …
The storm banged against the painted doors;
an undying rage that kept on going
in the darkness beneath the snow …
"Why are you here?"

"They say, those who go to church
are those who wanted to seek forgiveness, is it true?"

"Yes." The priest nodded wearily
as the effects of the poison slowly seeped
into the skin and the veins latched onto him
like a noose on the pedestal;
the intravenous drips festered the blood
and collapsed upon his weakly heart
where in moments
he felt that he was falling apart …
His eyes grew dimmer but the candlelights
and the silver cross that stood tall upon the altar
remained incessant and bright.

"I am a sinner. And I shall heap
coals of fire upon my head if my forked tongue
does protest … But I am guilty of another.
And no matter how I tried, it was in vow
that I will bear this burden upon my shoulders.
'Tis a curse I possess and its past does take its toll upon me

for leaving my family as I surrendered
myself to selfish desires. I know
that I will not be forgiven
and I shall embrace the punishment
that is bestowed upon me while performing my duties
to help those with the likes of me."

"I am not like you." The man stood up
and walked towards the podium, leaving behind
the rotten thing that dredged on the floor.
He eyed the stage and bathed in the spotlight;
he felt the heat on his back
and the rage he held on for so many years
dissipated like the sand in the hourglass.
The silver cross reflected the face of a stranger,
and the man could bearly recognize himself;
the man he has become. But here,
in this room, he was equal
as those that came before him,
praying for forgiveness from the evil
and sin that consumed one's beating heart.
His hands were tired and he took off the veil.
When the two guilty men turned to face each other,
they found how similar as they were different
in each other's eyes. And they were very similar.

As the storm continued its tolls beyond the wall,
a candle was lit outside the painted windows,

looking through the glass. And he was welcomed
by the candlelights and they did show him refuge.
The warmth, however, was never felt
and could only be just a blurry thing
that went along with the smoke in the shivery white mist …

"Why are you here?"
"I do not know."

"Then take whatever you want."

So the man took the silver cross and returned
to the darkness that kept him in
as the seventh chime rang
on this lonely bell tower,
calling out for the slightest err
of drunkards and thieves who lost their way.

Chapter 8

Eight Bells

It all started. The leeward winds blew ever so
gently from the bold mountain top.
And down the hill it went, the silent graves settled
upon cold callous valleys where words
travelled deep into the snow, branded on;
the calling of eight bells. The restless graves
clamoured underneath the old cypress yew
as the snow ebbed and flowed
like the recurrence of the distant sea.
Follow the wind and the tides below,
bury your thoughts in the deep deep snow.
Listen, as the eight bells sing those sorrows away
and shed solemn tears in a fortnight to forgive.

Listen.
Do you hear the voices in the snow?
It's here. Come closer.
Listen again. There is a lady in the snow.

She came from the town, not far from here—
Down there below, bathed in warm Christmas lights.
She advanced forward, braving through
the blizzard one step at a time.

For every inch it grew a little bit thicker
and darker but closer to the sky that reflected no stars.
It was a pit that was born from the dark,
reversed and extended upwards
as far as it could go. The cypress yew
hung on the bare ledge and looked down
at the little thing that came to visit;
she always welcomed a visitor. The lady in grey
sat underneath the shadows and watched
as the white and cold pictures moved before her eyes;
It all started. The tombstones whispered silently.
Do you hear the voices in the snow?

Listen. Listen again.
The roots ran deep beneath the graveyards,
deeper than any crevice that stood between the earth
and the old hanging tree. Listen …
The stones creaked one after another, breaking
and reassembling in the thawing snow.
If one could peer through
the layers of dried dust and bones,
one could see the markings that went on indefinitely
with names withering away in passing,
leaving behind silent waters that dripped along
the lines of unquiet neighbours …
The yew sang soft carols in the wind
as the wind rustled against its hollow veins.

There was a light in the horizon
far away from the bright town below.
The lady in grey could see it vaguely
but the currents made it audible and clear.
She would never take her eyes away
and would gaze at the distant sea,
waiting for a ship beyond the water's end.
Every day, the lady would take the same walk
to the cold mountains and stare
endlessly into the night … Eight bells,
and that was all she wanted to hear—
the time she knew her husband will return to her one day
but he never did. So she waited by the yew
on this Christmas Eve and prayed
for the celestials to guide his way.

But it all started when the sky was darkened and the storm
collapsed upon this blind and chaotic world.
The small town vanished in existence
and could never be seen from the mountain top.
The lady watched as everything returned
to a singularity of snow and white.
The lady could feel the snow growing under her feet
as she sank in slowly by the inch. But perhaps
something was emerging from the depths …
Her legs were chained and unable to move.
The cold deserts raged on and eventually,
the lady fell on her knees. Her hands were cold

and her heart was beating slowly …
The lonely creature weeped in broken words.
Listen.
Do you hear the voices in the snow?
Listen. Listen again.

The badlands reeked amongst white cobble and stone
and the sound of clamouring bones continued
in the snow. But there was one
by the old hanging tree
that sat quietly in the shade;
a peculiar headstone that spoke of no name.
It stared like an empty painting,
peeled off and aged in the senescent of time.
There were no words written on the stone
for there was no grave to stand watch.
And a headstone without a grave
is not a grave at all, only a slab
waiting to be weathered in the snow.
And yet it stood before her like a mirror,
wondered with bleeding pride.
It was the horror of it all
as the lady saw herself upon the empty slate
and wandered off
in her frenzied frame of mind.

The stalactites swayed upon the hanging tree
as they waited for their heavy fall.

The cursèd bones bellowed in the deep
and before the empty headstone
they mourned for that same moment
of what it seemed to be their destined end;
for it all starts and ends
with the dawn of first snow.

The lady shed her tears. And so she will
every day; in this night of Christmas Eve
and the many nights that is to come
until the snow turned to salt
and the salt to dust …
the match sat silently beside the grave.
Listen. Listen again.
Do you hear the voices in the snow?
The ship's horns rumbled in the distance.
Upon the wild pictures in the snow,
the world was silenced and lulled back to sleep.
Follow the wind and the tides below,
bury your thoughts in the deep deep snow.
Listen as the eight bells sing those sorrows away
and shed solemn tears in a fortnight to forgive.

The howling storm dissipated
and made a clearing upon the horizon.
The lady in grey held her heart
and glanced at the distant sea for one last time.
The snow fell gently before her eyes

as the beauty of the night withered away
along with the snow and the soil and the graveyard
that extended through the valleys.
The yew bid her goodbye
and the lady in grey treaded slowly
down the cold mountain top as the winds
returned to the seas in which where they came from.
Listen.
Listen again.
Do you hear the voices in the snow?

The eight bells rang at the center of town
and it shook the cold world amongst the snow.
The blind lady continued her anointed path
to wait for what was unknown and lost
as the light in her eyes slowly faded away
and the empty voices were all that was remained.

Chapter 9

The Forbidden Song

What was the last thing you remember?
What was the last thing you forget? Alas,
the pretentious poppies do let us remember
how delicate it is to be placed
upon the spectrum of time. Listen—
as the forbidden song flew and withered
amongst the snowy valleys; it was not a song
that we could remember
but of one that we tend to forget
as we covered ourselves with a painted veil
to conceal what flaws lay underneath.
And yet it stood under the spotlight
as it diminished to nothing
like a bulb that fades away
one day and loses its tungsten flame …
But it was the moment when all was left behind,
could we hear the faint utterances
of the 'forbidden' song
that was kept in passing time until
nothing remains but bitter snow and clattering bones …

The blizzard surged through the lonely gates
and casted its white shadow in the darkest alleys.

Its shackled grasp clasped upon the heart of town
where wishful kingdoms aligned;
the town people sang their prayers and hymns
in their little red houses and cosy warm beds.
And yet they too felt the cold air
escaping their lungs …
only the glass stayed unshaken in between
as the storm breathed upon its attenuated skin,
leaving behind willow patterns of crystalline frost.
And in this fervor night of Christmas Eve,
the elderly home sat amidst the warm and cold
as the world detached itself from existence
and succumbed to the demented state of mind.

The old man sat beside the one-eyed window,
and glanced at the many folk
that were joined together in this big common room;
Side by side like patients on hospital beds,
only darker and quieter with the absence of light.
For it was an abandoned old house
that redeemed no fortune or whatever
broken bits that were still yet to repair …
Strangers would come and visit, but only
sometimes when they put on familiar faces;
busy sons and distant daughters.
Nonetheless, it was home
for all tired and dying men alike.
There were those who stayed silent for months

and never closed their eyes. And others
who would laugh and talk to themselves ever so often,
but never work in proper conversations.
(If one were lucky,
the binding screws would still be
well intact. Most likely not.)
The barking dogs kept them away.

Why was he staring at the wall? Those ridiculously
overwhelming amount of holes
sticked out almost cancerous and impossible
to look at. And yet, the old man
was intrigued by the depths
and the many fine layers
that stacked up to create this spontaneous effect;
ripples frozen in white chalk and concrete
as if to capture that moment
of resonant beauty. Though 'beauty'
comes in different forms; and how would we know?
The old man focused on a scratch on the wall and followed
its tail that went far deep into the corner.
It was like a star that skid across the universe
and a casual crayon stroke
that a little boy made one silly afternoon.

"He likes it that way, look at him go!
Let him draw that picture.
Oh how lovely it is …"

The old man gently touched his hand
and slowly guided his fingers. Together,
they drew on the freshly-painted wall
and the air was lighter and full of color.

"A flower here,
A little kitten over there. Could you see it?
If you do it this way—
Yes, very good! A little bit more
curls here, and don't forget the eyes!
See how happy they are.
The little daisies that stayed in the meadows,
the tall magnificent pines, the little birds—
oh the little birds … I do miss those times."

"Grandpa, are you alright?
Who are you talking to?"
A little boy approached the lonely bed
and sat beside him on the wooden chair.
He placed a candle by the one-eyed window
and lit it with a match from his pocket.
The glowing little flame filled the empty room;
everything was clearer and came to light.
The room was smaller than expected
with the "Get-well soon" card sitting on the table
and the smell of lilies and daffodils
blooming from their little patches of grass
in handmade baskets. There was only one bed.

"My dear Michael, is it you?"
"No grandad, Father's not here.
I'm your grandson." "My dear boy,
then where is your father?"
"Father's busy at work."
"… Even on Christmas Eve?"
The old man lay down on his loyal bed
and stared at the ceiling. The storm continued
outside the strange and twisted world
and the room grew colder as the wind
seeped through the edges of the one-eyed window …
The snow knocked on the door.

The little boy held his hand
and shared the quiet moment with him.
He felt the weakly veins in his skin
and the dusted white chalk on his fingertips.
The little boy's hand gave him warmth
as the blood flew through his heart
and indeed, filled the empty spaces with those
beautiful memories that once kept him
fighting on for so long … to see his little boy
grow up, to be with him every step
and every granite he collected.
He helped him up on his upward battles
and watched as he became a father himself,
a loving father and gave him a beautiful grandson …

Oh how these memories flashed before him
like startling winds— Alas, it was so difficult
to return to those tangible moments
that gave him meaning; the love,
the happiness, the sorrows …
It only took a single tear and it was all gone.
The gentle bells rang at the center of town
as the world played its forgetful song
along with the snow that wilted away
into nothingness in which everything begins.
"Michael, are you here?" The last thing
the old man could ever remember
and only for a brief moment before nothing was left—
was a little boy holding his hand tightly
and the few wistful words that he whispered in his ear:
"Yes Father. I'm here."

Chapter 10

The Lost Chime

What was it that gave it color?
The snow that flutters in the wind,
as plain as it may be, the whiteness of it
does give it meaning— only momentarily
as it dwindled upon the frail and worn
in the distant town of Christmas Eve.
Where were the bits and pieces that were torn off
by the scorches of wind and the occasional
accidents of moving phantom cars
that didn't seem to care? The streets were dark,
showing the flesh beneath the cold brittle skin.
The bloodless creatures gnawed in the cracks
and were every so still, until
those living pores reached out for their precious air to breathe …

The streets were alive and the tall watchers
stood across the yellow brick road
with lights illuminating from their little cabinets;
dim and unaware but well enough for those
returning to find their way home.
But as you turn to the corner at the end of the road,
an estranged streetlamp was placed
awkwardly by the side, alone and unlit

in that cold patch of dark. For what monstrous pretence
lurked beneath those daunting shadows?
Mad worlds aside, it was just an ordinary streetlamp,
only older and out of time.

Where was the light that's kept its temperament?
The candle wick was dry
and the weakly spirit was long gone
before it had the chance
to be burned into white ashes in the snow.
The hollow thing that stood
in between was all that was left of it …
the foreboding rite has paid its visit.

The streetlamp was ancient,
scarred throughout long histories of time
with its skin peeled off, curled up
like splinters on the promontory;
the monument stands tall.
Its metallic pole was once a thing
of exceptional beauty with rare vintage designs;
the subtle curves subsumed the breath of the ingener
and the branches kept it in motion
as the air searched through its wavy patterns.
But when the skin was hardened,
rough scabs appeared on its knees.
It started off with a gentle graze
until it was untreated and became so unnatural

and infected like a vicious swarm. It grew.
Alas, the only thing he could ever wish for
was some foolish lad to turn the wrong corner
at the end of the empty road … A drunken fellow perhaps—
But who could have known? No one.
The black carnivorous mass
has devoured half of his body and he prayed
for the white snow to stay a bit longer this year
before the vile corrupted thing reaches the top …
The storm was kind. His prayers were answered.

The snow was colder than it was before,
the spirits numbed the unfettered soul.
The earth shook beneath the cradle
as the cackling bones continued
its calling in this cold cold night. The gentle snow
covered his rusted wounds and at least
for this brief unfeigned moment, the bleeding stopped;
Nature's poppies, oh bless her soul!
And yet why was he still standing there?
Wasn't it easier to lie down on the snow?
He didn't answer, only the will of it
as he forced himself awake
with shaky legs pushing against the heavy ground below.

His leg hurts. But he dared not to move.
It was just like the feeling
when one grew so tired and knees

too painful to bear that the right standing position
would cause him less harm. The only trouble was,
you need to keep it that way; But he didn't mind.
It was that sense of duty, I suppose, the purpose
of which he was forged and anchored
at this very peculiar spot. And so, he must.
But what was there to keep when one has no light?
Doesn't it end or does it continue like
a life sentence signed on cold parchment paper?
He smiled. Perhaps there was something greater in mind
for that he prayed and continued his watch
over that dark and unsettling place
he called Home. But who's to judge?
Alas, he was just an ordinary streetlamp
tucked away in Devil's keep.

It was hard to see through it all, the layers of snow
that stacked up against each other
showed only rare glimpses of the spaces in between.
But look closely enough and one could see
the frost sparkling in its faintest glow;
for the snow behooved the heavy soul
and bestilled the tears
that came flowing down from the crest.
It was more the reason to stay awake
as it was the only light he could ever see
with his half-blinded eye,
lest perchance an urge to sleep

and fall into some wicked snare
of waking again to see it disappear in the shadows …
The snow spoke of the heart.

Then it all stopped. Cold worlds
captured in polaroid frames
froze in a singular moment of time.
The streets were swept underneath their feathered beds
as the mistletoes swayed their wishful charms
behind the window glass, safe and undisturbed.
Beyond the receding storm, the silent figure
stopped by the end of the road
and looked into the corner where the old lamppost stood.
The snow was steady. The winds becalmed.
And there he saw the clear contours of its face
glowing ever so slightly as she came closer to him;
a silhouette of a little girl in her little red hood.

It's curious for one to venture these abandoned lands
and yet, those gentle footsteps do prove themselves
apparent and true. Was she real?
He was certain when she gave him
that honest smile so free of heart
and the words she whispered softly in his ear
did give him courage. For when she touched
his corroded skin, the putrid matter retreated,
revealing what possible beauty

that lay beneath the undercoat;
the starry reflections of stainless white silver.

She thanked him for the many nights
that he stood alone in the dark—
She thanked him for his duties
that kept heavy travellers away—
She thanked him for all there was bear
that gave him pains and heartless scorns …
But know that, on this Christmas Eve:
He was not alone tonight.

The light in his cabinet shone brighter than ever
for the little girl gave him her last wooden match.
As the sound of the tenth chime rang across the town,
there were no streets or corners stayed unlit,
only the little red cape was left silently in the snow …
and the little girl was now nowhere to be seen.

Chapter 11

The Little Match Girl

It was in those fretful seconds when the town
was submerged in a cold vicious brew
and of all things left unsaid and forgotten
did we pray upon our faintest recollection
to remember the moment that it all began.
For all that remained in ragged clothes,
the poor girl sat on the bench
and stared at the far town shrouded by snow.
The road stayed hidden underneath,
too deep into the snow for the little girl
to walk along those stone-tiled floors.
And in between the paths that led different ways,
she stayed on her bench, homeless and alone;
for the little girl had no name.
She watched in silence as those transparent shores
washed up away in the horizon and pondered
among all other things that are so easily to be forgotten.

What was in her mind? If only one could wonder …
Cold, yes, but her fingers never trembled.
She couldn't care less. Or perhaps she had never felt
that luscious feeling of warm homemade soup.
She could only dream. Alas, to feel out of place

in a world that she never belonged
was something that she grew very accustomed to.
The town was too bright for a little thing like her,
neither was she brave enough
to dredge through the snow
like the soldier boy who came walking
from the woods and passed by with steady march.
Where could he be going in this stormy night?
Not that it mattered anyway; for her eyes
have grown too tired to see and with it
came crashing down the weight of the snow.
She closed her eyes and slept
as the wind whispered soft breaths in her lungs.

There was an old lady on the bench.
The little girl woke up and found herself
startled by this unusual encounter. But the lady was kind.
She gave the little girl her red hooded cape
and a box of matches to keep her warm at night.
It was the greatest offer the little girl could ever have.
The little girl cradled the cape. She loved it.
So it came to a surprise when the little girl
took only one match from the box
and handed back the rest to the kind lady
along with the red cape she so dearly loved.
"One was enough for a little girl like me,"
she said, as she held onto her only match

and smiled in return.The worn-out threads
tethered on the side of her cheeks. The lady patted her head.

But the lady left the matches anyway and asked
the little girl to deliver them for her.
"To give light," she said, as she pointed
at the lights that were fading far in the distance ...
The little girl agreed with her kind little heart.
But before she could say anything else
the lady was gone, leaving behind
the red hooded cape and the box of matches
that sat there attentively on the cold wooden bench.

Twelve matches. Twelves destinations.
An errand that she gladly took. The little girl
placed those matches safely in her pocket
and went off into the storm in her little red cape.
She ran. Her legs were lighter than the winds
that chased behind her as she flew across the snowy plains
without the slightest chance to sink
into the deep deep snow— she closed her eyes
as the warm currents under her feet
kept her moving and afloat ...
The night was young. Her path was clear
and the snowdrops guided the way.

The little girl arrived at the town past the long empty road.
She came to a house of red, white and green

as the family of five celebrated together in this joyous
Christmas Eve.
There was no need for garments of fancy satin lace,
only simple bread and butter
was enough to read a mother's heart.
Then she came to another house, of one
that's abandoned and without color. The dried-out paint
laid beside the desk and the vacant chair
that faced directly at the coffin bed, cried in silent tears.
And the little girl in red lit the candles for each house;
one on the Christmas wreath that kept on knocking
and the other beside the wooden chair that made its faithful
vows.

Where would they take her now? The little girl in red
waited amongst the snow and found herself
wandering in the garden of dreams
where memories were buried deep into the snow.
And there she placed two matches on the lovers' bench
in hopes of a meeting that deserved a happy end.
Then it was halfway when she met an old man
sitting alone on the doorstep. But curious it was
to find herself in his place that reminded her
of the cold and nightmares that kept them awake.
So she stayed with the old man as the storm went by
and gave him a match that would perchance bring him peace.

Twelves matches. Seven more to go.
The cold air pressed against her chest as the little girl in red
came to a little shack at the farthest part of town.
It was said to be monsters that cackled in the night,
but what monsters would cry and be scared to live alone?
Alas, the simple man cried before the altar
at the holy chapel and could rid himself
from any name or senseless pride.
So as the candles stood in the lonely night,
the little girl lit them with her matches
that kept those nights unabating and alight.

The night was colder with the storm at its neck
and the frost in her breath started make it harder to breathe …
Almost there now. The little girl in red went up
to the mountains where the old graves were
as she left a match by the nameless grave
and prayed for the sailor to come back untroubled and safe.
And on the way down, she met a little boy
who stood at the porch in the withering snow.
He didn't move. He didn't know what to say.
The little girl in red gave him a match
and told him to be brave as he met
his ailing grandfather for one last time.

Then just before her final stop, she came to the streetlight
that was forgotten in the dark. Its light was unlit
with its skin splintered and scratched off like a broken torch.

"But it'll be alright," she said.

And the little girl in red began to climb.

She reached to the top and lit it with the match.

But then all happened too fast when the wind blew and a slip

of the feet made her lost her grip— She fell.

Dropped to the ground

like a dead

bird. Eyes staring

upwards. Paralyzed.

Drenched in the snow.

The night was clear and the heavenly lights

shone so brightly before her eyes.

Oh how warming it must be to the touch …

But she couldn't feel a thing now, nor could she see

under her red hooded cape. But it didn't matter.

She smiled at the snow that fell upon her cheeks …

The song of weeping bells rang through the town

as the last two matches laid separately on the ground

and one of which got snapped into two.

The little girl in ragged clothes closed her eyes

for the second time … and this time was indeed her very last.

Chapter 12

The Governor

Snow. Why does it creep like it's alive?
How is it more than just a form of precipitation
that falls upon the ground and crystallizes
whatever surface it touches? Or perhaps,
at least once was when it was given its first breath.
The silence continues and what lies beneath it
runs deeper than any mystery and stories untold.
As the repertoire of memories scattered across the town,
it is for one to capture these long lost tales
so that they could be remembered; an awakening
for those kept on living
but losing what it seemed to be
that gave them meaning in their lives.
For I am but a humble architect who amongst all other man,
spend their eternity
in search for those sentient voices in the snow.

I sit in my chair with my pen in hand
and looked at the town that is covered in snow.
Among the red houses that looked exactly the same,
there are those that stood out from rest.
Not necessarily fanciful stories or breathtaking adventures
that keep foreign ears well-attended, but

ordinary people with ordinary tales
that makes it heartfelt and refined to the slightest detail;
the one story that needs no alteration.
It is then when you found out that no red houses
look exactly the same, for the essence of it
lies within a half-emptied bottle and a broken screw.
I listen and to those that whispered in the snow.
They speak in the walls of hollow stones
and glamorous facades that turned out
to be extravagant and meaningless. But what is it
that gave them voice and the color
which kept them silent and still? The town is abuzz
and the restless storm roamed free in this cold winter's night.

Then it is at that moment when you stare
too closely at the window and realize the one person
you can hardly recognize in first glance;
the mirrored image of yourself.
There is always something different.
Perhaps a tear at the corner of your eye
or the bitter smile that you hide behind those cherry lips …
How often do you turn away to spare yourself
from all these translucent thoughts? This I am certain.
For it is in us to escape and forget
and to extend the reckoning that is long overdue
until we are so driven into madness
that we fall on our feet, knowing that it will come either way.

But the town will always be silent
and kept in time. You watch as the snow
moved freely in the air and lands on your window glass.
The light refracts upon all facets of the snow. It listens.
And that until you exhale your final words,
it takes its leave and dissolves into whispers that echo in the
night.
Perhaps you would hear a soft clicking in the snow. Listen,
as the carols take you back to when things were easier
and simpler under the old pine tree. Alas, we could all hope.
The fireplace shall keep us warm tonight.

The air is colder now and the town
is submerged in the hailing storm. For the snow
was not at all forgiving as I, too,
move away from the windows and start walking
in my room. The cold continues
as it seeps through the cracks and spaces beneath the doors.
I write on. Quivering in my own place,
I see the shadows lurking in the corners,
but none of which with ill intent.
For they are merely timid creatures
who are so often forgotten in dark …
who could be wandering in this stormy night?
The town withdraws into the snow
and the bitter word spread across the silent fields.

I am not cold anymore. The candle is lit beside my desk
and the fragrance does sooth my empty soul.
But I shall not take comfort
for there are those who move on in the snow,
bearing the winds that blow against their chest ...
It is in knowing that once you stop and lose your direction,
the storm will pull you backwards and the snow
shall gather around your feet, rooting you in place;
For that, you must tread on until those fingers
tremble no more. The snow will bring you home.
And so I shall become a deliverer of light as I open my doors
to weary travellers and those who lost their way.

The grief keeps me awake and how the longing
does haunt my every night that passes ...
But it is so easy to close your eyes
and never to wake up to the labyrinth
that seemed to lead on endlessly and repeatedly
every single day. For it is the pain
and loneliness that one must carry on to live
as we hang those dated pictures on those painted walls.
Emotions preserve in wooden frames and yet,
we see them age in fashion and lose their color
as we, too, lose our memories
one piece at a time ... The dust clouds our senses,
but the snow never forgets—
for the first snow will always fall on the day of Christmas.

The night is especially quiet upon in this hour,
but it is at its noisiest as you would pay attention
to little voices in your room. Listen and you would hear
the sizzling of the fire grasping for air,
the ominous creakings that never seemed to stop
as they accumulate and storm through your head
like a wild parade. Perhaps it's all in my mind.
And yet, my room did start to grow in size
and stretch out beyond those walls that contain me
as I sit in my loyal chair and the pen in my hand.

But there is always a chance to breathe.
The snowdrops whisper in the distance
as I arrive again to the garden of dreams and feel
the snow that falls upon my face.
The chapel still shines so brightly in dark
and it does keep my living nightmares away …
But alas, I am in my room and to those quiet nights I pray;
for I am certain that I hear a widow cry
and the ode of broken men weeping in the snow …
And yet who's to say that we are alone?
As the little match girl shall go from door to door
and light the candles at your porch. But I need no light.
For blight shall be my resting place
and the snow shall keep me safe.

And then for it my final word
to listen for the voices in the snow. The path is set

and it is for one to follow its course,
unknowing where it leads. Perhaps it's easier
to divert from the route and stumble into somewhere else
that has never been explored before.
A road, nonetheless, but darker and foggier
with your hands tied behind your back and eyes
blinded by the leaves and trees that got in your way.
You will bleed and it will only be for the bold and foolish.
Well, I chose the latter. Does it matter?
Alas, the tyranny of it all does keep us running in circles …
But there is something in the snow as the soldier boy
travelled far away to find himself back at the doorstep.
Home, and among all others that will find their way
returning to this forgotten town. The snow remembers.
And I will place my pen on the side of my desk
as I wait for the twelves chimes before Christmas
to echo across the town; for the twelfth chime
will be my very last … and it is for once,
shall I reside amongst the snow
and the town
where I truly belong.

Acknowledgements

Thank you to my dearest friends, Himeshika Samaradivakara, Jasmanpreet Kaur, Jennifer Liu and my beloved sister, Angela Chan, who have never stopped supporting me and inspiring me for the past year. I treasure every advice you have given me and the precious times you have taken out to proofread this book.

Thank you to my college teachers, Kate Rogers and Cicy Tong for encouraging me to strive for what I love to do, to write. I learned to be persistent and brave in facing whatever hardships and challenges ahead. You show me that it is possible to pursue my dream as a poet and a writer, and that here I am.

Thank you to my secondary school teachers, Fiona Li, Kadence Leung, Candice Ng and Cyrus Chow for introducing me to the world of Literature, and at the same time, giving me the most important push in my life that made me who I am now.

Thank you to my mother, Claudia Woo, for being the best parent I could ever have. I will never forget the stories and life lessons you have taught me and that I build upon these many perspectives to explore the world in my own eyes.

Last but not least— I want to thank all the people around me, my many friends and teachers who accompanied me in this life journey, and this book, is dedicated to all of you. For the stories

I wrote in this book, I wrote out of the lessons and experiences I had with every single one of you, and it has been the most rewarding and remarkable journey. And it is for my final word:

For I am but the servant
that brings these stories to life
with the pen in hand
that holds the cartridge of my humbled soul.

Orion Blightman

CPSIA information can be obtained
at www.ICGtesting.com
Printed in the USA
BVHW080238110119
537596BV00001B/118/P